Cleversticks

First published in hardback in Great Britain by HarperCollins Publishers Ltd in 1992
First published in paperback by Picture Lions in 1993
10 12 14 16 18 20 19 17 15 13 11
ISBN: 0 00 663855 4
Picture Lions is an imprint of the Children's Division,
part of HarperCollins Publishers Ltd.
Text copyright © Bernard Ashley 1992
Illustrations copyright © Derek Brazell 1992
The author and illustrator assert the moral right to be identified
as the author and illustrator of the work.
A CIP catalogue record for this title is available from the British Library.
The HarperCollins website address is: www.fireandwater.com
Printed and bound in Singapore

Cleversticks

BERNARD ASHLEY

ILLUSTRATED BY DEREK BRAZELL

Collins

An imprint of HarperCollinsPublishers

Ling Sung started school on Monday, but on Wednesday morning he decided he didn't want to go any more.

There were too many things the others could do that he couldn't. Like tying up his shoes. Terry could do his and he kept undoing them and doing them up again while everyone had to watch.

Ling Sung tried to do his but his fingers got tangled up and the laces kept going their own ways.

Manjit knew how to write her name. She wrote
it on all her things and she painted it on her
paintings even bigger than the picture.

Ms Smith and Mrs Dhanjal gave her a clap
and she held it up for everyone to see.

Ling Sung tried to write his name too. But he wasn't sure how to do the letters or which way the writing had to go.

The one thing Ling Sung could do came at home time. Very carefully he buttoned up his coat. But when he finished he had a button over and his coat was all up on one side.

Sharon did hers perfectly and Ms Smith said wasn't she clever? She didn't say anything about Ling Sung but just did up his coat properly while she talked to Sharon's dad.

Ling Sung didn't want to go to school ever again. He wanted to spend the whole day doing things he liked. Watching the Red Nose clowns in the park. Doing head over heels for the cat.

Splashing his mum at the pool.
And bathing his little sister.

But the next day there he was at school again. At biscuit time Anis showed everyone how he could tie up his overall at the back, all by himself.

Ling Sung couldn't even do up the apron with the Velcro tabs. He turned his back on everyone. He was fed up with clapping other people for the things they could do. Why couldn't he be good at something too?

He saw two long paint brushes. Someone hadn't put them in their jar.

Ling Sung fiddled with them and didn't pay
attention when the biscuits came round.
He nearly dropped his plate and his biscuits
broke in pieces.

Terry pointed at him and laughed. "You looked like a clown juggling that plate," he said.

"Red noses!" said Ling Sung – and made a clown face. He put both the brushes into one hand and chopsticked the biscuit pieces into his mouth – the way he ate at home.

Ms Smith suddenly clapped.

"Oh, look everyone! Look what Ling Sung can do! Isn't that clever?"

She was really pleased.

"Do it again, Ling Sung. Can anyone else use chopsticks?"

No one could.

"Oh, where's the camera?" said Mrs Dhanjal.

Ling Sung knew just how to hold the chop-sticks, and how to hold his plate close to his mouth. When he was small it had been hard to do, but now he didn't even think about it.

Everyone wanted to be shown how to do it.
It wasn't easy.

"Show us again Ling Sung," they shouted.

Ling Sung helped the teachers too. They were dropping biscuit all over the place.

They laughed and tried again.
"I can nearly do it," said Ms Smith.

Then Ling Sung got them to show him how to do their best things. Manjit helped him with his writing.

"Down and along," she said. "That's an L, and S for Sung is one big snake."

Terry showed Ling Sung how to do his laces.
"Round like this – and don't let go!"

And Sharon told him how to do up his coat properly.

"You don't start in the middle. Start top or bottom, then go down or come up. Easy."

Anis did up Ling Sung's apron for him –
so tight he could hardly breathe.

Ling Sung couldn't wait to tell his dad when he met him after school. He could do something for the others to clap!

"A real cleversticks!" his dad said.